Butterfly Garden

by Debra Hershkowitz

Harcourt

Orlando   Boston   Dallas   Chicago   San Diego

Visit *The Learning Site!*

www.harcourtschool.com

I have loved butterflies all my life. When I was
little, I never missed the chance to point one out.
Sometimes it was a real one floating past me outdoors.
Sometimes it was a picture in a magazine. When I
went to the library, I looked at books about butterflies.
Just seeing them made me happy.

Every year, the zoo in our city had a butterfly
house. I never missed it. In the butterfly house it was
very warm. Butterflies were everywhere. There were
shiny blue butterflies and creamy yellow ones. There
were butterflies with wings like colored glass windows.
There were butterflies with dots, and some with stripes.

When I got older I enjoyed biology in school. What is biology? Well, *bio-* means "life" and *-ology* means "study of." So *biology* is the study of life. Some biologists study plant life. Some biologists study marine life, or life in the ocean. I wanted to study butterflies.

I was also interested in taking pictures, so I began to study photography. I hoped that some day I would become a nature photographer. I would photograph living creatures, big and small.

Since I loved butterflies, I wanted to photograph them. I came up with a plan to "grow" butterflies in my backyard. That way I could photograph them as they grew.

How do you grow butterflies? First, you have to plant a garden. It can't be just any kind of garden. I found out what kinds of butterflies lived near my house. Then I found out what kinds of flowers those butterflies liked. Some of them liked daisies. Some of them liked day lilies. Some of them liked flowers I didn't know the names of. I even found a plant called a "butterfly bush" that attracts butterflies.

Every time I visited friends with gardens, I carried a big spoon and plastic bags with me. When I saw the kinds of flowers that butterflies like, I asked my friends for seeds or a bulb. Sometimes they gave me a whole plant.

After I planted the flowers, I was curious to see what would happen. A few butterfly visitors came that first year. I was so glad to see each one. I noticed a pale yellow butterfly that went only to my yellow daisies.

As I watched the butterflies, I learned a lot about how they grow. Butterflies don't start out as butterflies. They go through changes. Before becoming the beautiful creatures we know, butterflies make four changes.

First, there is an egg. Next, the egg hatches into a caterpillar. Then the caterpillar turns into a pupa. Finally, the pupa becomes a butterfly.

Of course, these changes don't happen quickly. Seeing them at the very moment of change is not easy. After a while, though, I got to be good at guessing when a butterfly was ready to hatch.

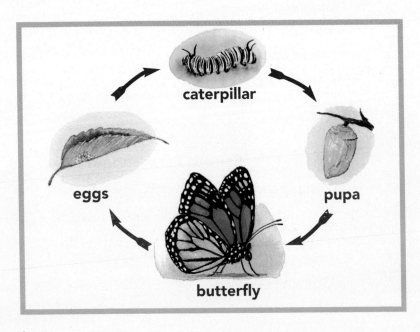

caterpillar

pupa

butterfly

eggs

I looked for butterfly eggs under the leaves of some of my plants. They were hard to find because they were so small. It was easy to miss them. Then one day I saw little yellow dots that looked like tiny pearls. They were butterfly eggs!

Now I could begin taking photos. I could hardly wait to see my pictures. When I saw them, I wasn't very happy. The eggs looked so small that they were almost invisible. I discovered what the problem was. I needed a different tool for the job.

The lens on my camera was good for shooting some things. It was good for taking close-up pictures of butterflies. It was not good for taking pictures of tiny butterfly eggs. I needed a special lens called a macro lens.

I took my camera to the store where I bought it. They had a macro lens that fit my camera. Now I was ready. I went home as fast as I could. There was still enough light to take my first macro lens picture.

The macro lens would let me focus up close. I could take a big picture of tiny butterfly eggs.

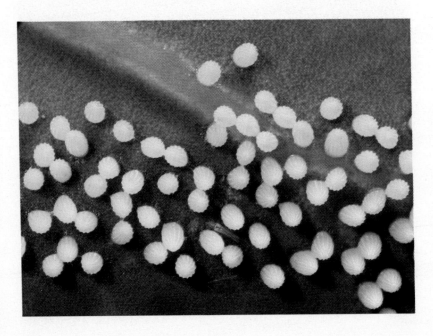

Another problem I discovered was shadows. Shadows made dark places on my pictures. I learned that even in bright sunlight, I had to be careful. I did not want a shadow on a bright butterfly.

I learned that sometimes it's better to shoot in the early morning. It should be bright but not too sunny. I also learned that I could use a flash to control the light in my pictures. I had to practice a lot to use the flash correctly.

In a few days, I watched one of the eggs hatch into a small caterpillar. This is the larva stage of a butterfly's life. Caterpillars are very hungry. They eat like crazy! Guess what the caterpillar's first meal is? It eats the eggshell it hatches from!

Eating is a caterpillar's main job. I discovered that a caterpillar eats more than its own weight in food in one day!

I was glad I had learned to use the close-up lens. My pictures were getting better and better. Every day I became a little more skillful.

My first photos of the caterpillar were just okay. The pictures looked different from what I had imagined. I thought the whole caterpillar would be in focus and look sharp. But it didn't come out that way in the picture.

This was another lesson. When I use a small lens opening, more of the picture will look sharp. When I use a large lens opening, only the thing I focus on will look sharp.

When the next roll of film came back, I was much happier. I was getting to be a better photographer.

I watched my caterpillar for two weeks. It stayed on the same plant, eating and eating. This was good, because it gave me time to practice. I took pictures every day.

The caterpillar ate so much, it grew fast. But its skin didn't. The caterpillar shed its old skin and grew a larger one. It did this several times. When it had grown as big as it would ever get, it shed its skin for the last time. Instead of growing another skin, it grew something else.

Now it was time for another change. It was time for the caterpillar to become a pupa.

The caterpillar found a nice spot on a twig. It attached itself with a sticky liquid from its body. Then it hung upside down from the twig.

Right away, the pupa started to form a hard shell. It looked like it was resting, but it wasn't! Amazing things were happening inside. The hungry caterpillar was changing.

I could hardly wait to see the next stage. I wasn't always sure exactly what kind of butterfly would come out. I knew, though, that whatever came out would be beautiful.

After a while the pupa began to break open. I stayed right there and shot photo after photo. I was so tired I almost collapsed, but I didn't give up. I wanted to have a picture of everything that happened.

Little by little, the pupa was opening. At last, a beautiful orange butterfly started to come out. Slowly, very slowly, it stretched its legs and unfolded its delicate wings. It was still a little wet and needed to dry off. After about an hour it was ready to fly.

Soon, there were lots of butterflies in my backyard. They left their twigs and started to take off. I loved looking at them, just as I did when I was a child. This time I understood so much more. They had been born in my backyard, and I hoped they would stay. I hoped they would survive in my butterfly garden.

Today I am the nature photographer I always wanted to be. I photograph many kinds of creatures, big and small. My photographs appear in books and magazines.

I will never forget that first year, though. I learned so much about butterflies and about taking pictures. I still love butterflies, and I still take pictures of them—right here in my butterfly garden.